ANIMALIA

For you Jesse,
to enjoy.

Barbara Berger
1982

ANIMALIA

Thirteen small tales
Retold, handwritten, & illuminated
by

BARBARA
BERGER

Celestial Arts • Millbrae, California

Celestial Arts

231 Adrian Road

Millbrae, California 94030

Library of Congress Cataloging in Publication Data

Berger, Barbara, 1945 Mar. 1-

Animalia: thirteen small tales

Summary: Brief tales of wise and holy people who have lived gently with animals from various countries and cultures including tales of St. Francis, Buddha, Siddhartha, and other European and Oriental legends.

1. Tales. 2. Legends 3. Animals—Folklore.

. [1. Folklore 2. Animals—Fiction.]

1. Title

PZ8. 1. B4163An 1982   398.2   82-9521   AACR2

ISBN 0-89087-342-9

First Printing, September 1982

Manufactured in Italy

1 2 3 4 5 6 7 8 88 87 86 85 84 83 82

Lovingly dedicated
to Kari

Breath, life, and soul were known as "anima" in Latin. Our word "animal" comes from this. There are always people who live in harmony with Animalia, kingdom of the animals. Many have been saints and sages who live in legend still. Each of these thirteen small tales is a bit of their old lore retold.

DUET

Rose was in the garden when she heard the nightingale. She echoed with a song of her own. The bird sang again, and Rose sang too, in her turn. Thus they passed the hour, singing an antiphonal duet. Rose let the nightingale sing the last soaring notes. Then the bird flew to her open hand. Rose said softly, "Your song has no compare. Are you an angel in those plain feathers?" The nightingale shook himself and vanished. Only silent light was left for Rose to hold.

Saint Francis walked from place to place with care. Often he saw a small creature in the road: a beetle, an earthworm, a spider or a snail, a centipede, or a lazy toad. He would bend down and gently lift the little being to the roadside, far from the way of horse's hoof and wagon wheel. There he would let it go. "Peace be with you, Little Brother," he would say.

DRAGON'S EYE

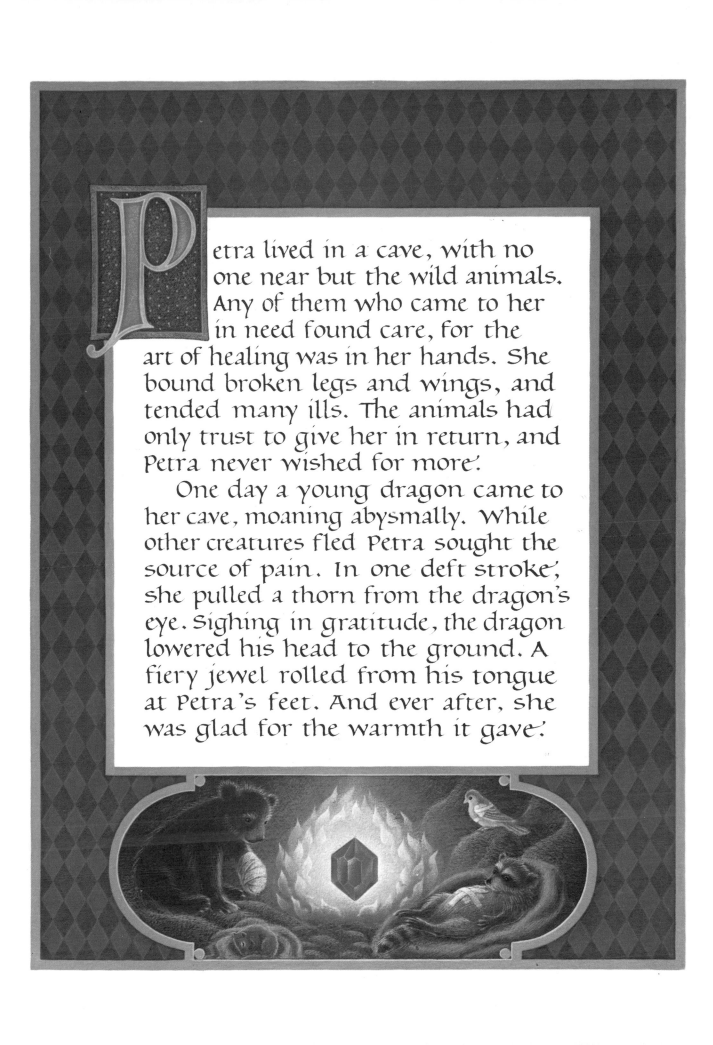

Petra lived in a cave, with no one near but the wild animals. Any of them who came to her in need found care, for the art of healing was in her hands. She bound broken legs and wings, and tended many ills. The animals had only trust to give her in return, and Petra never wished for more.

One day a young dragon came to her cave, moaning abysmally. While other creatures fled Petra sought the source of pain. In one deft stroke, she pulled a thorn from the dragon's eye. Sighing in gratitude, the dragon lowered his head to the ground. A fiery jewel rolled from his tongue at Petra's feet. And ever after, she was glad for the warmth it gave.

Brother Benno was walking along, chanting his prayers. He came to a marsh where the frogs were chanting too. Their sound was so great that Brother Benno could not hear himself. So he said in a loud voice, "Be still!" And they were.

In the stillness, Brother Benno began to feel very small. He thought, God might enjoy the chanting of these frogs more than my prayers. So he said to the frogs, "I am sorry for being so rude. Please go on singing as you wish."

One by one the frogs began to croak. Soon they were a choir of sound again. And Brother Benno listened.

THE
FLY

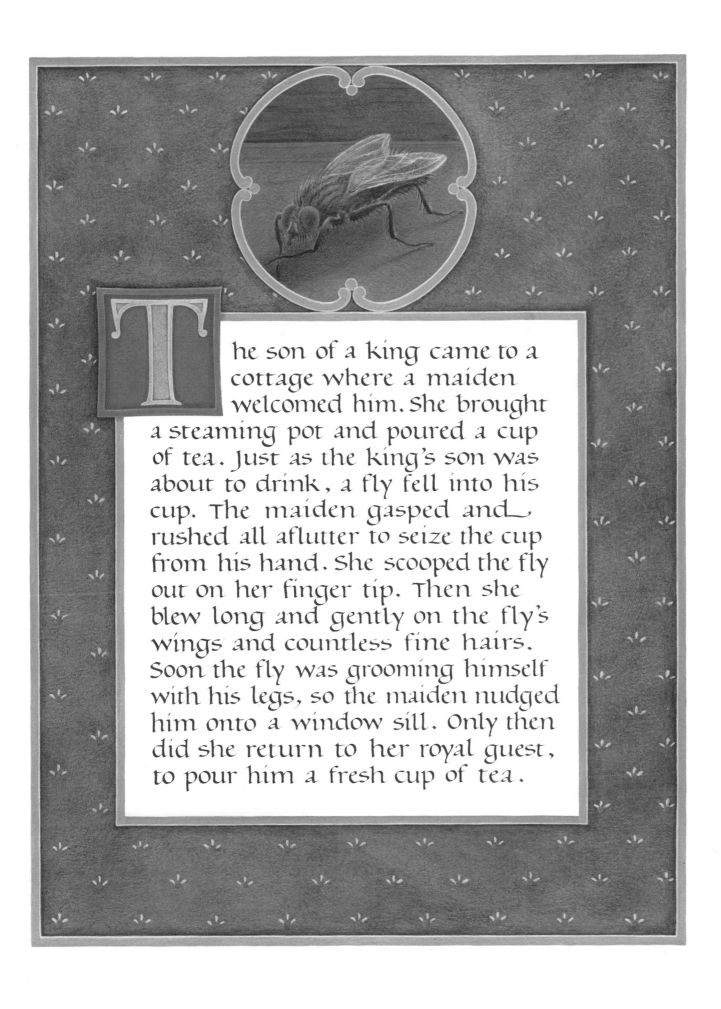

The son of a king came to a cottage where a maiden welcomed him. She brought a steaming pot and poured a cup of tea. Just as the king's son was about to drink, a fly fell into his cup. The maiden gasped and rushed all aflutter to seize the cup from his hand. She scooped the fly out on her finger tip. Then she blew long and gently on the fly's wings and countless fine hairs. Soon the fly was grooming himself with his legs, so the maiden nudged him onto a window sill. Only then did she return to her royal guest, to pour him a fresh cup of tea.

HAPPY GOLDFISH

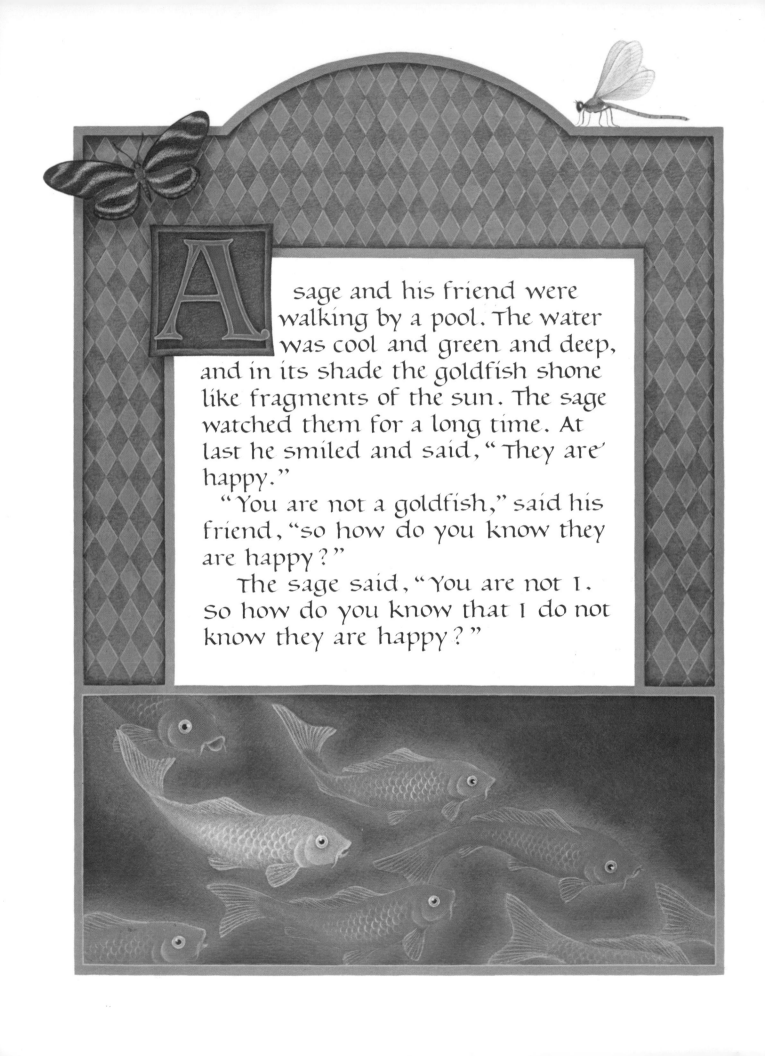

A sage and his friend were walking by a pool. The water was cool and green and deep, and in its shade the goldfish shone like fragments of the sun. The sage watched them for a long time. At last he smiled and said, "They are happy."

"You are not a goldfish," said his friend, "so how do you know they are happy?"

The sage said, "You are not I. So how do you know that I do not know they are happy?"

SISTER
HARE

Oringa was lost in the forest one night. Fear gathered the shadows around her heart. But all she could do was sit down among roots to wait the darkness through.

A hare came toward her, tall ears turning to every sound. But hares live in the open, not in a forest. Oringa whispered, "Sister Hare, are you lost too?" Calm as the moon, the hare came and settled in Oringa's lap. And the long night passed in the comfort of her company.

At dawn, Oringa followed the hare. She led between shadows and over roots, into the open, and home again.

DREAM

Once upon a time, a philosopher fell asleep. He dreamed he was a butterfly. From flower to flower he fluttered in the bright air. Resting at the center of each one, he unwound his spiral tongue to taste the nectar there.

Then the philosopher awoke. He asked himself, "Was I a human being asleep, who dreamed he was a butterfly? Or am I now the butterfly asleep, who dreams he is a human being?"

There was a monk who lived by the sea, where the breath of distant whales sounded near. He would stand in reverence all night in the waves, and otters came to play around his feet.

By day he went out in a little boat. If a whale came close, he calmly thought, we are made by the same hand, you and I. Once, he dropped his book overboard.

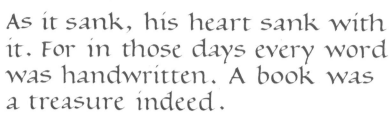

As it sank, his heart sank with
it. For in those days every word
was handwritten. A book was
a treasure indeed.

Before long, an otter brought
the book alongside. The monk
reached down and found his
treasure dry. Not a single word
was washed away. Then the otter
was gone, leaving only a ripple
upon the waves.

DOVES

In China, there was a prince who showed his kindness by setting doves free. Once a year, the air was filled with beating wings. But a tear shone on the cheek of his bride, and the prince asked her why.

"Dearest," she said, "the doves are freed because they are caught, and they are caught for you to set them free. But in the nets, wings and necks are broken. Many doves die."

So the prince ruled that doves were never more to be captured in his land. Every year they came freely, in a splendor of beating wings, to coo in peace upon the palace roof.

THE STAG

eep in the forest, St. Godric lived alone, his hut hidden in briars. One day he heard a horn and the baying of hounds on the hunt. Suddenly, a stag bounded to him, magnificent and trembling. Godric led the stag into his hut. Then he came out, shut the door, and sat down.

Soon a frenzy of hounds surrounded him, but Godric was still. The dogs could not get by him. When the hunters came they asked, "Where is the stag?"

Slowly Godric opened his eyes. "God knows where he may be," he said.

This is a holy man, the hunters thought, and a holy man does not lie. So they gathered their hounds and left. When the forest was safe again, Godric opened his door, and the stag was free.

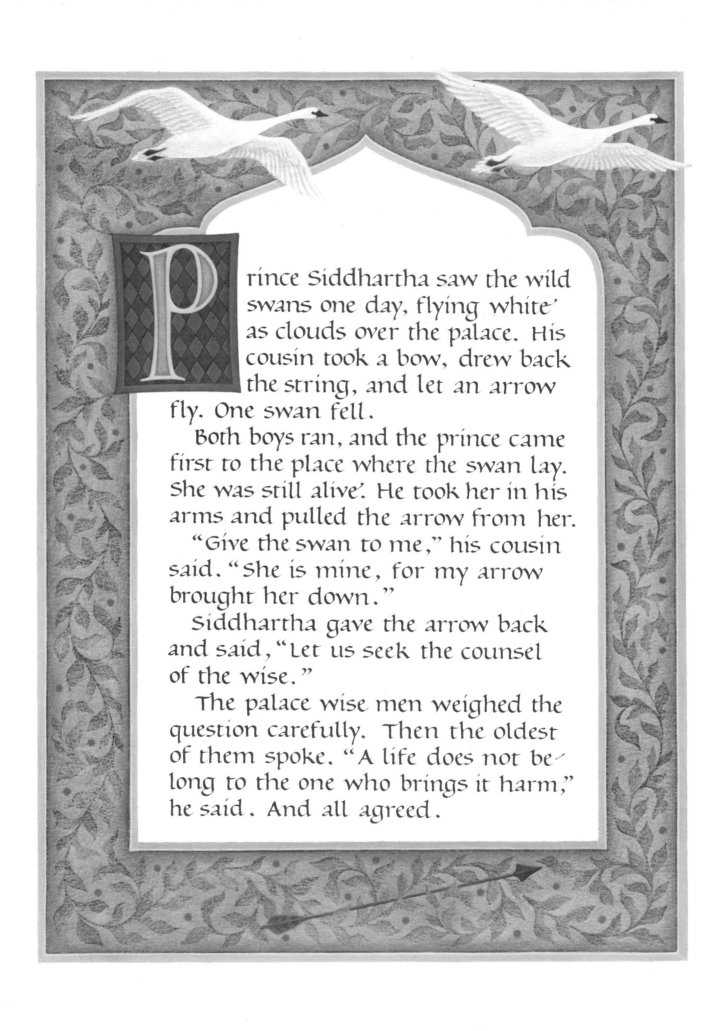

Prince Siddhartha saw the wild swans one day, flying white as clouds over the palace. His cousin took a bow, drew back the string, and let an arrow fly. One swan fell.

Both boys ran, and the prince came first to the place where the swan lay. She was still alive. He took her in his arms and pulled the arrow from her.

"Give the swan to me," his cousin said. "She is mine, for my arrow brought her down."

Siddhartha gave the arrow back and said, "Let us seek the counsel of the wise."

The palace wise men weighed the question carefully. Then the oldest of them spoke. "A life does not belong to the one who brings it harm," he said. And all agreed.

So the swan remained in Prince Siddhartha's care. And when her wound was healed, he rejoiced to see her fly again.

THE
TURTLE

ong ago, a sage came to a great river. There was no bridge, and no boat to carry him across. So he walked along the shore.

Soon he found a large turtle in a trap. The turtle's shell rose like a dome of jade. The sage knew this was a being far more ancient than himself. He set the turtle free.

At the water's edge the turtle waited, looking back at him with a timeless eye. The sage understood. He stepped up on the turtle's shell. The turtle swam out into the river, bearing the old man in steady grandeur to the other shore.

These stories were found in books about the saints,
books of Chinese tales, and the story of
Buddha's life. Some have been retold with little
change. Others have been freely embellished
and adapted in the retelling.
In the days before the printing press,
books were handwritten and often "illuminated"
with painting. The paintings in Animalia
were done in acrylic on fine watercolor paper;
the calligraphy was done separately in ink.
Both were then reduced.
Color separations, printing, and binding were done
by Amilcare Pizzi, s.p.a, in Milan, Italy.
My warmest appreciation goes to all at
Celestial Arts, especially Orly Kelly, Editor of
Children's Books and Abigail Johnston, Art Director.

B.B. 1982